Little Flower

A JOURNEY OF CARING

by Laura McAndrew
illustrated by Nancy Conrad

CWLA Press • Washington, DC

Dedication

To my mother, B. D. McAndrew, on the occasion of her birthday, with inexpressible love and thanks for the tender care with which she raised a certain little flower.

To all the children for whom home has not been a safe place, and especially those we have cared for at Sheltering Arms and Helping Hand Home— I wish you time to heal, room to grow, and lots and lots of love.
—L.M.

To the children at the KW House of Tiny Treasures.
—N.C.

CWLA Press is an imprint of the Child Welfare League of America. The Child Welfare League of America (CWLA), the nation's oldest and largest membership-based child welfare organization, is committed to engaging all Americans in promoting the well-being of children and protecting every child from harm.

CHILD WELFARE LEAGUE OF AMERICA, INC.
440 First Street, NW, Third Floor, Washington, DC 20001-2085
E-mail: books@cwla.org

CURRENT PRINTING (last digit)
10 9 8 7 6 5 4 3 2 1

Book design and production by S. Dmitri Lipczenko
Printed in the United States of America

Library of Congress Cataloging-in-Publication Data
McAndrew, Laura
    Little Flower / a journey of caring / by Laura McAndrew; illustrated by Nancy Conrad.
        p. cm.
    Summary: Little Flower, a potted daisy who is neglected by her family, finds help and a new place to stay until the people she was living with can learn how to take better care of her. Includes projects to help the healing process of those in a similar situation.
        ISBN # 0–87868-714-9 (alk. paper)
        [1. Flowers—Fiction. 2. Child Abuse—Fiction.]   I. Conrad, Nancy, ill.   II. Title
PZ7.M1177L1   1999
[E]—dc21   98-46960   CIP   AC

Once upon a time, there lived a beautiful
young daisy called Little Flower.

For as long as she could remember, Little Flower had lived in the same chipped clay pot on the same kitchen ledge, by the same shiny pots, the same tiny window, and the same noises of water running and pans clanging.

Little Flower knew that kitchen very well, for she had never left it. When she strained her daisy face to the tiny window, she could see nothing beyond it but a big green bush. Nothing could see in, either.

Because she was a young daisy, Little Flower
needed plenty of water to drink, sunshine to
breathe, and room to grow in her pot.

But often, the people in the house forgot to give her water to drink.

And she couldn't reach most of the sunshine
that came in the tiny window.

And she didn't have room for all her roots
in her little pot.

Little Flower wished she had more water to drink, more sunshine to breathe, and more room to grow. But most of all, she wished someone would spend time with her and love her.

The people in the house seemed to care about her, sometimes, but then they would forget. This made Little Flower very sad.

Sometimes, when she was sure no one was watching, Little Flower cried. The tears ran down her petals and into her small pot.

Little Flower hung her face down in shame.

She thought no one would love her when she looked like this.

Little Flower could not see that she was still very beautiful, even though she looked sad and thirsty.

One day, the people of the house went on a trip.
They told Little Flower goodbye, and said they
would see her again soon.

Little Flower did not know where they had gone
or when they were coming back. She missed them.
Little Flower became thirsty, because she had no
water. She felt lonely and scared.

As time went by, Little Flower felt more lonely, and more scared, and more sad. Little Flower couldn't cry anymore.

    One day when she was feeling very sad, Little Flower heard something.

    She heard a noise from the window. Tap, tap, tap. With all her strength, she arched her little face up and saw a beautiful red robin looking right at her.

"Are you okay, Little Flower?" asked the robin.
At first, Little Flower didn't answer.

Little Flower was sure the robin would think that she was a bad flower, and that the people had left her by herself because she was bad.

But Little Flower did not want to be alone anymore, so, in a very brave way, she looked right at the robin and said, "No, I'm not okay. The people left me here and there's no one to take care of me. And I feel very lonely, and very scared, and very sad."

The red robin, who was a wise and kind bird, said, "That was very brave of you to tell me. You need someone to care for you. I will go find help and return soon."

Little Flower still felt lonely and scared, but now she also felt something nice. She felt hope. She shook out her leaves and petals, wanting to be ready when the robin came back.

Soon the robin came to the window, and
a nice woman with lots of curly brown hair
went to the back door.

The nice woman knew that there was a
young flower inside who was hurting, so she
had a police officer in a uniform with shiny
gold buttons help her get the door open.

The nice woman came in and smiled at Little Flower.

Little Flower smiled back, just a little.

The nice woman said, "Little Flower, some people haven't learned how to give flowers what they need. I will help the people you live with learn how to care for flowers. But until they learn that, you need to live in a place where other people can give you what you need.

You need water to drink, sunshine to breathe, plenty of room to grow, and lots and lots of love. I know just the place."

The nice woman picked Little Flower up and took her to another house.

Little Flower met the man and the woman and the little boy who lived there.

The nice woman said, "These people will take good care of you," and soon she left.

Little Flower missed her other house and the people in it. But she looked forward to the visits the nice woman promised would take place when they returned from their trip.

Slowly, Little Flower got to know the people in her new house. They took good care of her. She had lots of water to drink, sunshine to breathe, and a big new clay pot to grow in.

Best of all, she had lots of love.